the **BAD GUYS**

# • FOR MY BOYS •

TEXT AND ILLUSTRATIONS COPYRIGHT © 2015 BY AARON BLABEY

ALL RIGHTS RESERVED. PUBLISHED BY SCHOLASTIC INC., PUBLISHERS SINCE 1920, 557 BROADWAY, NEW YORK, NY, 10012. SCHOLASTIC AND ASSOCIATED LOGOS ARE TRADEMARKS AND/OR REGISTERED TRADEMARKS OF SCHOLASTIC INC. THIS EDITION PUBLISHED UNDER LICENSE FROM SCHOLASTIC AUSTRALIA PTY LIMITED. FIRST PUBLISHED BY SCHOLASTIC AUSTRALIA PTY LIMITED IN 2015.

THE PUBLISHER DOES NOT HAVE ANY CONTROL OVER AND DOES NOT ASSUME ANY RESPONSIBILITY FOR AUTHOR OR THIRD-PARTY WEBSITES OR THEIR CONTENT.

NO PART OF THIS PUBLICATION MAY BE REPRODUCED, STORED IN A RETRIEVAL SYSTEM, OR TRANSMITTED IN ANY FORM OR BY ANY MEANS, ELECTRONIC, MECHANICAL, PHOTOCOPYING, RECORDING, OR OTHERWISE, WITHOUT WRITTEN PERMISSION OF THE PUBLISHER. FOR INFORMATION REGARDING PERMISSION, WRITE TO SCHOLASTIC AUSTRALIA, AN IMPRINT OF SCHOLASTIC AUSTRALIA PTY LIMITED, 345 PACIFIC HIGHWAY, LINDFIELD NSW 2070 AUSTRALIA.

THIS BOOK IS A WORK OF FICTION. NAMES, CHARACTERS, PLACES, AND INCIDENTS ARE EITHER THE PRODUCT OF THE AUTHOR'S IMAGINATION OR ARE USED FICTITIOUSLY, AND ANY RESEMBLANCE TO ACTUAL PERSONS, LIVING OR DEAD, BUSINESS ESTABLISHMENTS, EVENTS, OR LOCALES IS ENTIRELY COINCIDENTAL.

LIBRARY OF CONGRESS CATALOGING-IN-PUBLICATION DATA

NAMES: BLABEY, AARON, AUTHOR.
TITLE: THE BAD GUYS / AARON BLABEY.
DESCRIPTION: NEW YORK: SCHOLASTIC PRESS, 2016. | ©2015 | "FIRST PUBLISHED BY SCHOLASTIC AUSTRALIA PTY LIMITED IN 2015." | SUMMARY: THE BAD GUYS, MR. WOLF, MR. SHARK, MR. SNAKE, AND MR. PIRANHA, WANT TO BE HEROES, AND THEY DECIDE THAT THE WAY TO DO IT IS FREE THE 200 DOGS IN THE CITY DOG POUND—BUT THEIR PLAN SOON GOES AWRY.
IDENTIFIERS: LCCN 2015037847 | ISBN 9780545912402
SUBJECTS: LCSH: ANIMALS—JUVENILE FICTION. | RESCUES—JUVENILE FICTION. | HEROES—JUVENILE FICTION. | CYAC: ANIMALS—FICTION. | RESCUES—FICTION. | HEROES—FICTION. | HUMOROUS STORIES.
CLASSIFICATION: LCC PZ7.B52864 BAD 2016 | DDC [FIC]  DC23
LC RECORD AVAILABLE AT HTTP://LCCN.LOC.GOV/2015037847

10 9 8                    17 18 19 20 21

PRINTED IN THE U.S.A.   23
FIRST U.S. PRINTING 2017

# · AARON BLABEY ·

# the BAD GUYS

SCHOLASTIC INC.

GOOD DEEDS.

WHETHER YOU LIKE
IT OR NOT.

# · CHAPTER 1 ·
# MR. WOLF

Pssst!
Hey, you!

Yeah, you.

Get over here.

I said, **GET OVER HERE**.

What's the problem?

Oh, I see.

Yeah, I get it . . .

You're thinking, "Ooooooh, it's a big, bad, scary wolf! I don't want to talk to him!

He's a **MONSTER**."

Well, let me tell you something, buddy—
Just because I've got

**BIG** POINTY
TEETH

and

**RAZOR-SHARP**

**CLAWS**

. . . and I *occasionally* like to dress up
like an **OLD LADY**, that doesn't mean . . .

...I'm a

# BAD GUY.

# METROPOLITAN
# POLICE DEPARTMENT
## SUSPECT RAP SHEET

**Name:** Mr. Wolf

**Case Number:** 102 451A

**Alias:** Big Bad, Mr. Choppers, Grandma

**Address:** The Woods

**Known Associates:** None

**Criminal Activity:**

* Blowing down houses (the three pigs involved were too scared to press charges)

* Impersonating sheep

* Breaking into the homes of old women

* Impersonating old women

* Attempting to eat old women

* Attempting to eat relatives of old women

* Theft of night gowns and slippers

**Status:** Dangerous. DO NOT APPROACH.

It's all **LIES**, I tell you.

But you don't believe me, do you?

Because I'm the Bad Guy, right?

I'm a great guy. A *nice* guy, even.

But I'm not just talking about **ME** . . .

I've got some buddies who have the same problem, so I've asked them to join us.

Any minute now, they'll be walking right through that door.

They're great guys. But just like me, they are **MISUNDERSTOOD**.

So don't go anywhere, OK?

## · CHAPTER 2 ·
# THE GANG

OK. Are you ready
to learn the truth?

You'd better be, baby.

Let's see who's here,
shall we?

*Heeey!* Look who it is!
It's my good pal,

# MR. SNAKE.

You're going to *love* him.
He's a real . . .

. . . sweetheart.

# METROPOLITAN POLICE DEPARTMENT
## SUSPECT RAP SHEET

**Name:** Mr. Snake

**Case Number:** 354 22C

**Alias:** The Chicken Swallower

**Address:** Unknown

**Known Associates:** None

**Criminal Activity:** * Broke into Mr. Ho's Pet Store

* Ate all the mice at Mr. Ho's Pet Store

* Ate all the canaries at Mr. Ho's Pet Store

* Ate all the guinea pigs at Mr. Ho's Pet Store

* Tried to eat Mr. Ho at Mr. Ho's Pet Store

* Tried to eat the doctor who tried to save Mr. Ho

* Tried to eat the policemen who tried to
save the doctor who tried to save Mr. Ho

* Ate the police dog who tried to save the
policemen who tried to save the doctor
who tried to save Mr. Ho

**Status:** Very dangerous. DO NOT APPROACH.

Look at this face!
Is this the face of a monster?

I don't think so.

This is **ONE SWEET GUY**.

Will this take long, man?
I've got mice to eat.

**HA HA HA HA!**

What a joker this guy is!

"I've got mice to eat!"
That's a good one.

What a wise guy.

**HA HA HA.**

**HA.**

**HA.**

Take it easy.
Have a cupcake.

A cupcake?
You got
any mice?

Enough with the mice,
or I'll

EAT
YOU!

I mean . . .

Well, well. If it isn't
# MR. PIRANHA.

Now, if anyone has
a bad reputation,
it's this guy . . .

*Hola.*

# METROPOLITAN POLICE DEPARTMENT
## SUSPECT RAP SHEET

**Name:** Mr. Piranha

**Case Number:** 775 906T

**Alias:** The Butt Biter

**Address:** Tropical Rivers

**Known Associates:** The Piranha Brothers Gang, 900,543 members, all related to Mr. Piranha

**Criminal Activity:**

\* Eating tourists

**Status:** EXTREMELY dangerous. DO NOT APPROACH.

I've come all the way from Bolivia, *hermanos*.

And I'm hungry! So where's the

MEAT?

HA HA!
These guys are killing me! Always with the jokes!

No meat.

Just cake.

KNOCK! KNOCK!

AHA!

Now I know **THIS** guy likes cake . . .

KNOCK!

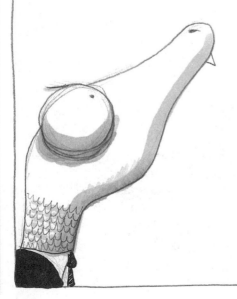
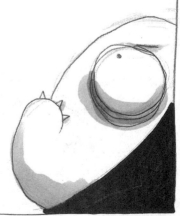

Hey there, **MR. SHARK**.

How's it going?

I'm

# HUNGRY.

You got any seals?

Okey dokey. Nothing to see here . . .

# METROPOLITAN POLICE DEPARTMENT

## SUSPECT RAP SHEET

**Name:** Mr. Shark

**Case Number:** 666 885E

**Alias:** Jaws

**Address:** Popular Tourist Destinations

\* Will literally eat ANYTHING or ANYBODY.

RIDICULOUSLY DANGEROUS. RUN!
SWIM! DON'T EVEN READ THIS!

**Status:** GET OUT OF HERE!!

See?! This is what I'm talking about!
How will anyone take us seriously as

# GOOD GUYS

if all you want to do is

# EAT EVERYONE?

What am I **TALKING** about?

Well, sit down and I'll explain.

And that means *you*, too.

# · CHAPTER 3 ·
## the
# GOOD GUYS
# CLUB

AAAAHHHHHHH!!!!!!

Typical . . .

Hey, shouldn't you two be in water?

I'll be wherever I want.

Got it?

Me too, *chico*.

See? This is why
I don't work with fish.

**44**

I beg your pardon?

You heard me.

Aren't you tired of being the
**VILLAIN?**

Aren't you tired of the
**SCREAMS?**

Aren't you tired of the
**FEAR?**

Not particularly.

Not in the
slightest.

# OF COURSE YOU ARE!

And I have the solution!

**POP QUIZ!**

Let's say we find a cat stuck in a tree.

What do we do?

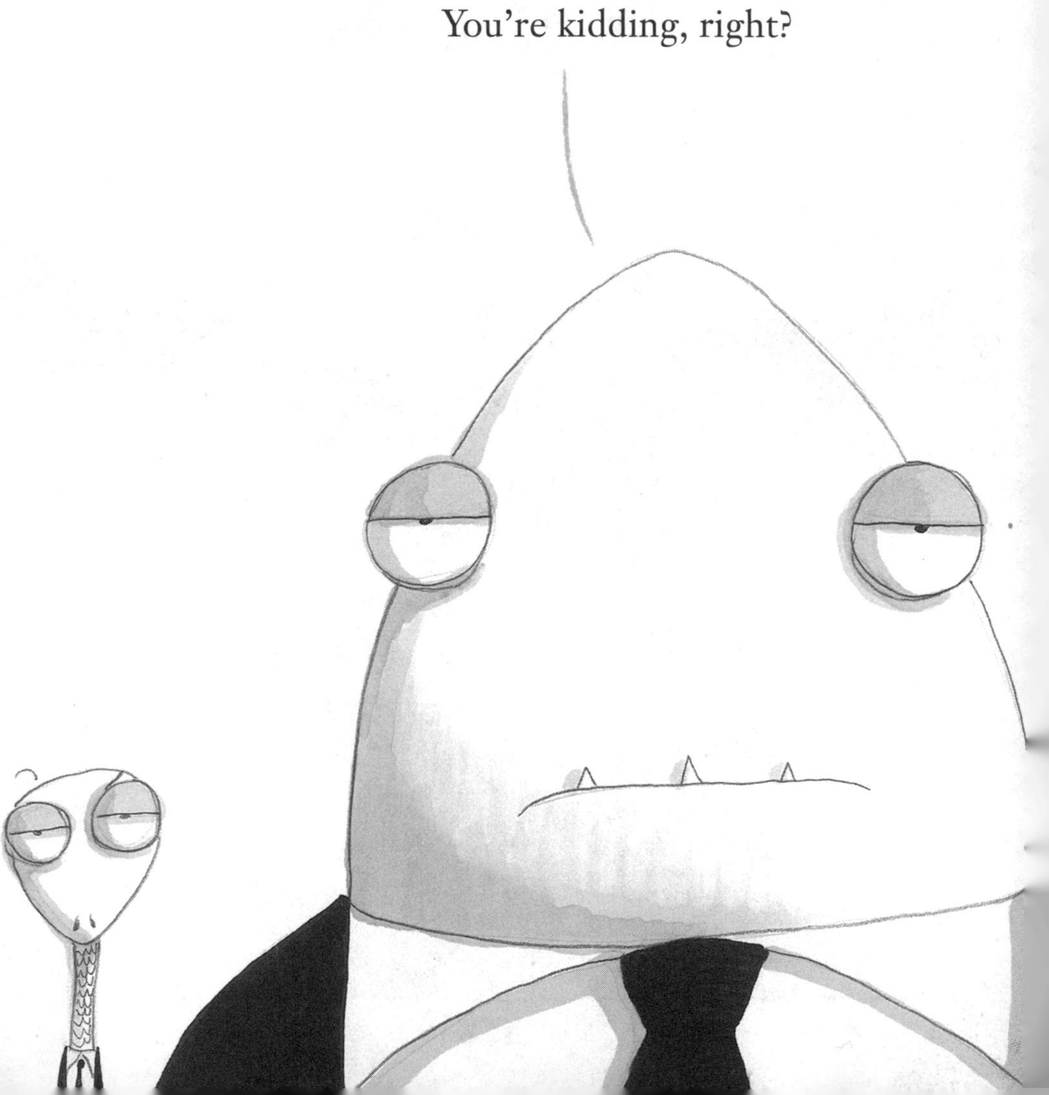
You're kidding, right?

This guy's *loco*.

# No, I'm not!

## I'm a **GENIUS!**

### And I'm going to make us all

# HEROES!

He's completely lost his mind.

I came all the
way from Bolivia
for THIS?

You'll be glad you did, Mr. Piranha.

And so will you, Mr. Shark.

This is going to be **AWESOME**.

Now, everybody climb aboard!

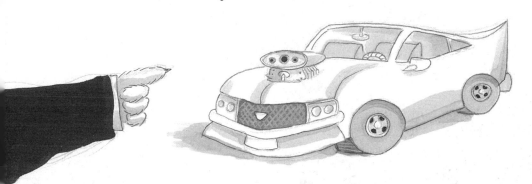

And let's go do some

# GOOD!

# · CHAPTER 4 ·
# CRUISING FOR TROUBLE

This car is a fuel-injected, **200-HORSEPOWER**, rock 'n' rollin' chariot of flaming **COOLNESS**, my friend. If we're going to be good guys, don't you think we should **LOOK GOOD**, too?

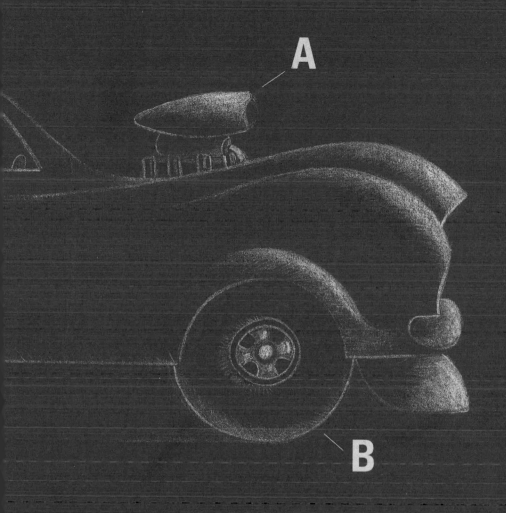

A - Wicked powerful V8 engine that runs on undiluted panther wee.

B - Fat wheels for just looking insanely cool.

C - Custom ejector seats for personal safety and also practical jokes.

D - Oversized muffler for being very, very loud at all times.

And it's roomy, too!

Hey, it's a sweet ride, *chico*. But I get carsick, man. So, what ARE we doing out here?

We need to
be able to
**SMELL**
trouble!

In fact . . . wait a second . . .
I think I can smell trouble
right now . . .

Wow, it's really strong, actually . . .

Hang on. That's not . . .

AW, WHO FARTED?!

HEY!

What's the big deal, *chico*?
Car travel makes me
let off a little gas.

SO WHAT?

Actually, that feels real nice.

Seriously though, man . . . what are we looking for?

SCREEECH!

**THAT** is what we're looking for, Mr. Snake!

# · CHAPTER 5 ·
# HERE, KITTY

So, what are we going to do?

Rescue the cat.

And what are we **NOT** going to do?

Eat the cat.

**THAT'S RIGHT!**
I don't know about you, but I feel PUMPED!

OK, now let's do this thing . . .

Meow?

Here, **KITTY, KITTY, KITTY!**

HERE, KITTY, KITTY!

EEEEEEEE!

What was *that*? Are you trying to give him a heart attack?

WHAT? I was, like, being totally cool . . .

Let me handle this.

# HEY, YOU!
Get down here, or I'll **SHIMMY** up that tree and **BITE** you on your **FURRY LITTLE BUTT!**

What's the matter with you?!

Well, someone had better do something. That screaming is getting on my nerves . . .

MUNCH!

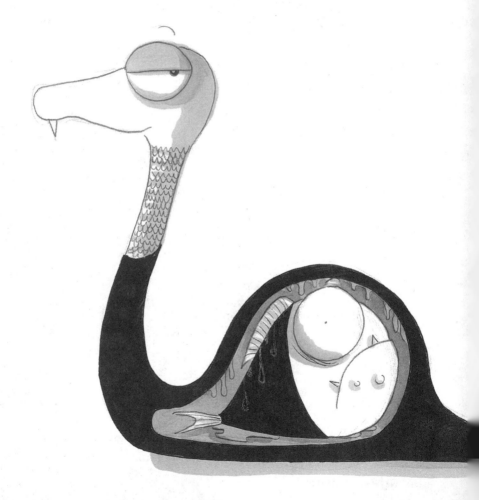

**NOW,**

please don't be **alarmed.**

# It's true,

snakes can be tricky and they do tend to

**swallow** whatever they like.

BUT—luckily, they swallow things *whole*

and I happen to know a **gentle,**

harmless technique that'll fix this right up.

Excuse me for **one** moment . . .

I SAID . . .

WHERE'S

THE
PIRANHA?!

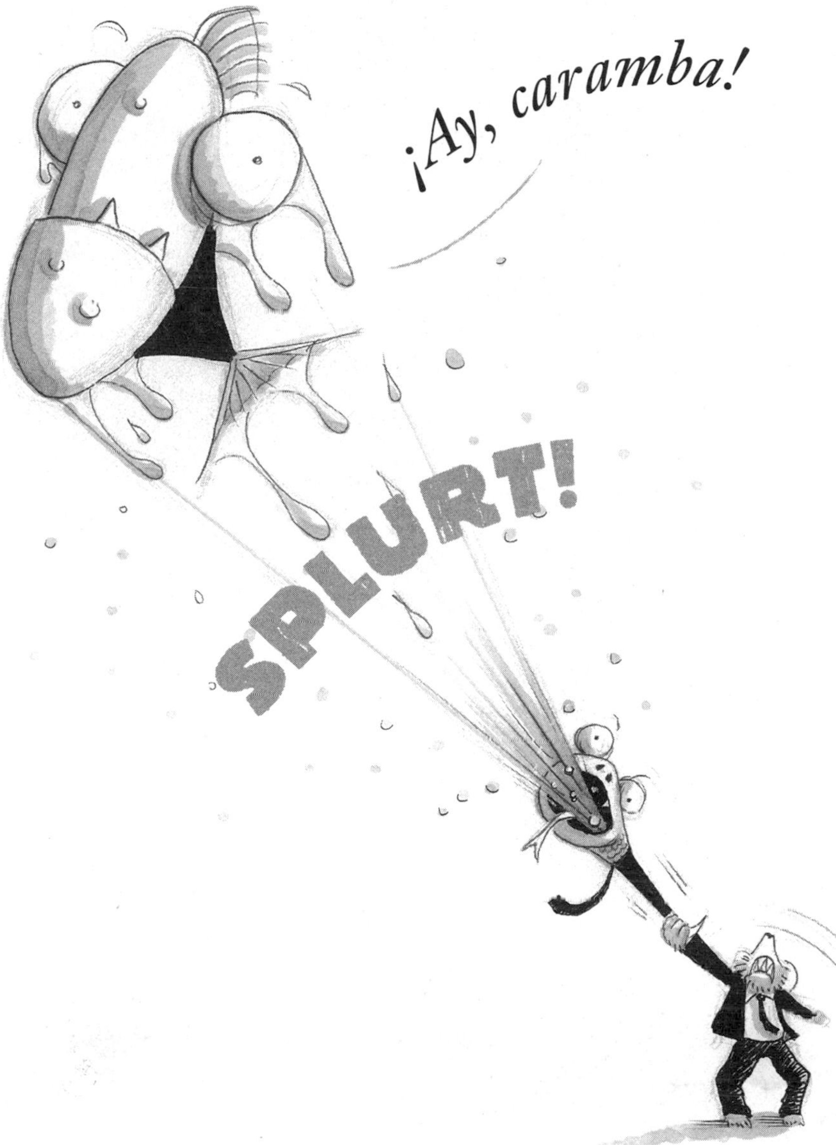
¡Ay, caramba!
SPLURT!

Hey, *chico*.
What's cookin'?

# · CHAPTER 6 ·
# THE PLAN

Nice work.
High fives,
all around!

You're the only
one with hands.

Fair enough.

**GROUP HUG?**

I don't hug. I bite.
So **BACK OFF**,
Mr. Snuggles.

Okey dokey . . .

Ready for what?

Well, I don't
know about you,
but I'd say we're
**READY**.

Our first mission.

It's time for
**OPERATION DOG POUND!**

THE

200 DOGS

534

10

# DOG POUND

20 GUARDS

ONE WAY IN.
ONE WAY OUT.

IRON BARS!
RAZOR WIRE!
BAD FOOD!

There are **200** puppies locked up in the

## MAXIMUM SECURITY
## CITY DOG POUND.

Their hopes and dreams are trapped
behind walls of stone and bars of steel.

### But guess what?

We're going to

SET THEM FREE!

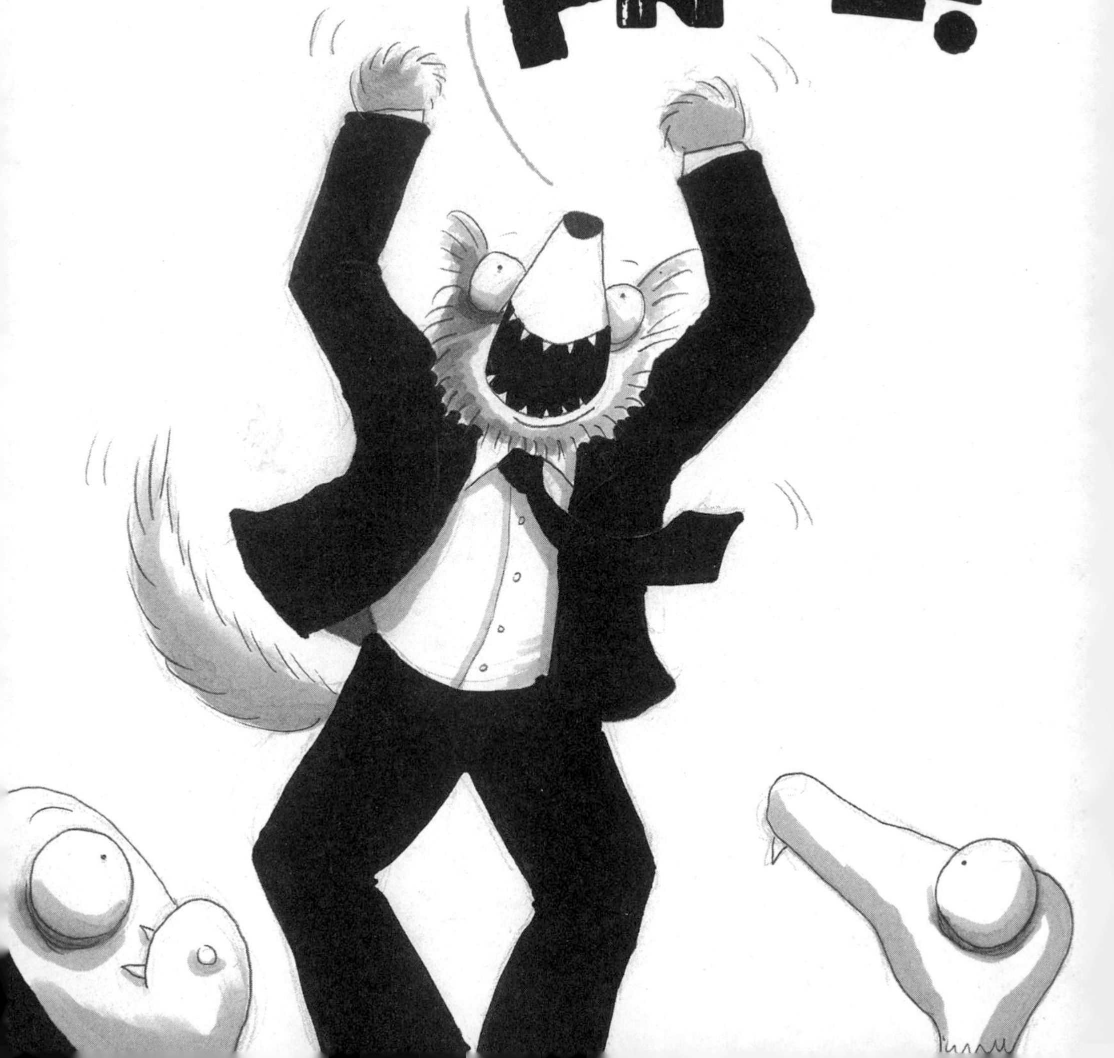

We couldn't get a kitten out of a tree. How are we supposed to bust out 200 dogs?

It's easy! One of us just has to get in there and open the cages!

And how do we do that?

Are you going to dress up like an old lady AGAIN? It doesn't work, man. You ALWAYS get caught!

Who said anything about *me*?

# · CHAPTER 7 ·
# THE POUND

Hello?
Oh, certainly, miss.
I'll buzz you in.

BUZZZ!

Now, what can I do
for . . . uh . . . you?

I'm just a pretty young lady who has lost her dog.
Please, oh please, can you help me, sir?

# Well,
## OF COURSE!

Anything for such a
lovely young lady.

Cool.

He's in!
I **KNEW** this
would work.

Now, you know what to do.
Once those cages are open,
we won't have long,
so don't mess it up.

Climb aboard, fellas!

What's that
thing for?

Never mind. Just hold on tight.
And remember—once Mr. Shark
gives me the signal, I'll get you
inside and all you have to do is tell
the dogs which way to run.

## GOT IT?

Yeah. But
how do we
get inside?

But don't worry!

I have **EXCELLENT** aim

and I'm **85%** sure

that I'll get you in on my first throw—

**THAT'S**

how confident I am!

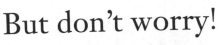

Well, here's the last cage.
Is THIS your dog?

**NO!** Oh, woe is me!
I shall never find
my dog!

OH, BOO HOO! BOO HOO!

There's no time to talk! Hold on tight, little buddies.

It's time . . .

to go

BE A HERO!

SWOOSH!

OK.
Best out of three.

**YEAH.**

I'm getting the
hang of it now . . .

SPLAT!

I'm sorry, young lady, but I'd better lock these cages back up now.

THIS. IS. GOING. TO. WORK.

If we survive this, I'm going to *eat* that wolf.

WHOOOSH!

Not if I do first.

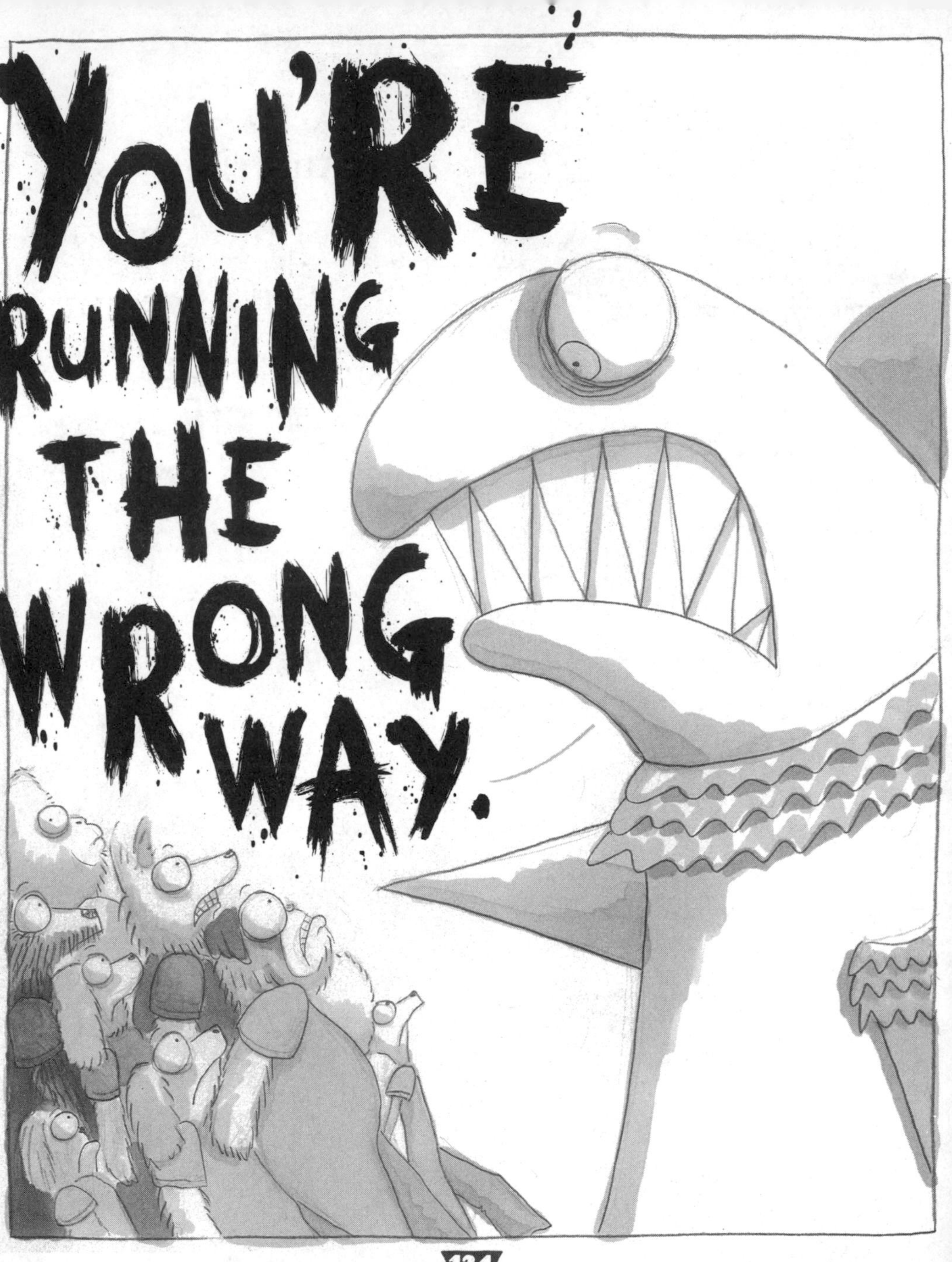
YOU'RE RUNNING THE WRONG WAY.

I hear you,
little buddy.

Let's give those puppies their . . .

# · CHAPTER 8 ·
# SO, HOW ABOUT IT?

Well, they certainly didn't seem very grateful, did they?

They called me a SARDINE!

I thought you WERE a sardine.

I'm not a SARDINE! I'M A PIRANHA, man! **PIRANHA!**

Whatever.

You're missing the point, guys. **WE DID IT!** We gave 200 dogs a whole new life. Doesn't that make you feel **AWESOME?!**

You really do hug WAY more than I'm comfortable with, man.

Aw, **C'MON!**
You loved it! I KNOW you did!
Tell me the truth—didn't it feel great
to be the **GOOD GUY** for once?
Tell me how it felt, fellas . . .

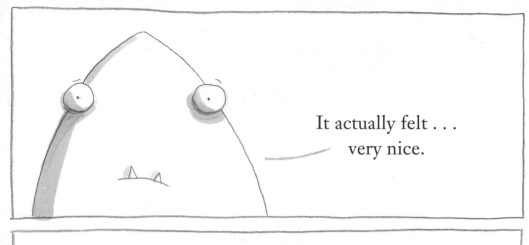

It actually felt . . .
very nice.

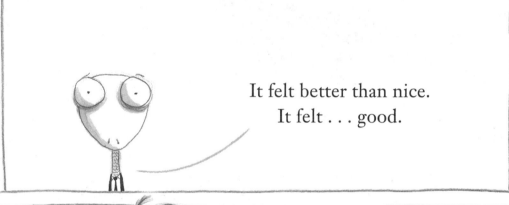

It felt better than nice.
It felt . . . good.

It felt **WONDERFUL**, man.
But they still called me a SARDINE!!!

If you stick with me, little buddy, no one will ever mistake you for a sardine ever again! You'll be Bolivia's most famous hero! Are you with me?

Sure. But you'd better be right, *chico*.

And what about you, big fella?

I . . . I really liked being good. I'm in.

That just leaves you, handsome.
What do you say? Want to be
in my gang?

Only if I have your word that
there'll be no more hugging.

I'll try, baby! But I'm not
making any promises!

Today is the first day of our **new** lives.

We are **not** Bad Guys anymore.

# WE'RE GOOD GUYS!

And we are going to make the world a **better** place.

# TO BE CONTINUED . . .

# GUESS WHAT?

The **BAD GUYS** haven't even warmed up.

Freeing 200 dogs is **NOTHING**.

How about rescuing **10,000 chickens** from a **high-tech cage farm** protected by the world's most **unbeatable** laser security system?

BUT how do you rescue chickens when one of you is known as **The Chicken Swallower?**

Join the **BAD GUYS** when they return for more shady **good deeds** with a new, creepy member of the team . . . and keep your eyes peeled for the **SUPER VILLAIN** who just might be the end of them.

Look for the **BAD GUYS** *in Mission Unpluckable!*

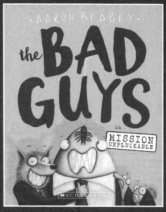